This book belongs to …

....

Tips for Talking and Reading Together

Stories are an enjoyable and reassuring way of introducing children to new experiences.

Before you read the story:

- Talk about the title and the picture on the cover. Ask your child what they think the story might be about.
- Talk about what it's like to travel on a plane. Has your child ever seen a plane or been to an airport?

Read the story with your child. After you have read the story:

- Discuss the Talk About ideas on page 27.
- Look at the pictures of things you might pack in your bag on pages 28 – 29 and talk about what you would take on holiday.
- Do the fun activity on page 30.

Have fun!

Find the pairs of sunglasses hidden in every picture

For more hints and tips on helping your child become a successful and enthusiastic reader look at our website **www.oxfordowl.co.uk**.

Going on a Plane

Written by Roderick Hunt
and Annemarie Young
Illustrated by Alex Brychta

OXFORD
UNIVERSITY PRESS

"Hooray!" yelled Dad. "We've won a holiday in the Canary Islands. We'll fly out and stay in a four star hotel near the beach."

"We've never been on a plane before," said Biff.

"Or stayed in a hotel," said Chip.

"I can't wait!" said Kipper.

"Thanks, Floppy!" said Dad. "The competition was on your dog food packet and we won."

"Good old Floppy," said Biff."

"We'll go at half term," said Mum. "We can't take
Floppy with us, but Gran will look after him."

"He'll like that," said Chip.

At last it was time to pack.

Biff had too many clothes. "You don't need that many," said Mum.

Kipper had too many toys. "You can't take all of those," said Dad.

Chip got it right. "T-shirt, shorts, a hat and a book," he said.

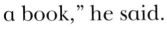

They went to the airport on a coach ...

... they had to wait to check in ...

… they handed over their bags …

… they showed their passports. Kipper had made one for Ted.

They went through security. Kipper's bag had to go through an X-ray machine – and so did Teddy.

"Don't get lost, Ted," said Kipper.

At last it was time to board the plane. Kipper was excited. The plane was really big.

"This plane is massive," said Kipper. "It has so many seats."

"These are ours," said Mum.

Everyone wanted the window seat.

In the end, they let Kipper sit by the window.

"Get your books and games, and settle down quickly," said Dad.

The flight attendant was called Guy. He gave the children a pack of things to do.

"It's a long flight," said Guy.

"Fasten your seatbelts and make sure the seat is upright," said Guy. Then he told everyone what to do in case of an emergency.

"Will you hold my hand when we take off?" said Mum. "I get scared."

"All right," said Kipper. "I'm not scared. It's exciting."

After a while, the flight attendants gave out food on little trays.

"I'm not very hungry," said Biff.

"Well I am," said Dad.

At last the plane landed. "That wasn't so bad," said Mum.

Their passports were checked.

They got their bags. "Now to find our hotel," said Dad.

They saw a minibus. "This one will take us to the hotel," said Dad.

The minibus driver stopped at a hotel. "Here is your hotel," he said.

"Oh no!" said Mum.

The hotel looked terrible. It was old and dirty.

"Look!" said Kipper. "This isn't our hotel. The picture is different."

"Kipper is right," said Dad. "This *is* the wrong hotel!"

Just then a taxi came along. Mum waved and it stopped.

Mum asked the driver if she could take them. She
showed her the address of their hotel.

"Get in," said the driver.

"This is better," said Mum.

"Well done, Kipper!" said Dad. "This is going to be a great holiday, after all."

Talk about the story

Why was everyone pleased with Floppy?

What did the family do before they got on the plane?

How did Kipper know they were at the wrong hotel?

How would you most like to travel on holiday?

What would *you* take on holiday?

Which of these things do you think Kipper took on holiday?

Which ones can you find in the pictures of the story?

What would you take on holiday?

Teddy

Wellington boots

sunscreen

passport

camera

Floppy

watering can

umbrella

hat

book

t-shirt

Find the right minibus

Which minibus has this picture on it?

First Experiences with Biff, Chip & Kipper

Have you read them all yet?

Kipper's First Pet

Learning to Swim

Going to the Dentist

Going to the Doctor

Going to the Hairdresser

Fun at the Farm

Going on a Plane

Starting School

FIRST EXPERIENCES Flashcards
55 cards

Also available:

- Kipper Gets Nits!
- At the Hospital
- At the Optician
- Bottles, Cans, Plastic Bags
- On a Train
- At the Vet
- At the Match
- At the Dance Class

Read with Biff, Chip and Kipper
The UK's best-selling home reading series

Phonics

First Stories

	Phonics	First Stories
Level 1 Getting ready to read	Kipper's Alphabet I Spy Chip's Letter Sounds Biff's Wonder Words Floppy's Fun Phonics	Get On Floppy Did This! Up You Go Six in a Bed
Level 2 Starting to read	I am Kipper Cat in a Bag The Red Hen The Fizz-Buzz	Funny Fish Silly Races! The Snowman Dad's Birthday
Level 3 Becoming a reader	Such a Fuss Shops The Sing Song The Backpack	Poor Old Rabbit I Can Trick a Tiger Super Dad Floppy and the Bone
Level 4 Developing as a reader	Wet Feet The Moon Jet The Red Coat Quick! Quick!	Missing! The Raft Race Dragon Danger The Spaceship
Level 5 Building confidence in reading	Egg Fried Rice Craig Saves the Day Seasick Dolphin Rescue	Hungry Floppy Husky Adventure Trapped! Looking after Gran
Level 6 Reading with confidence	Gran's New Blue Shoes Ice City Save Pudding Wood Uncle Max	Hairy-Scary Monster Mountain Rescue The Lost Voice Secret of the Sands

Phonics stories help children practise their sounds and letters, as they learn to do in school.

First stories have been specially written to provide practice in reading everyday language.

READ WITH Biff, Chip & Kipper

OXFORD
UNIVERSITY PRESS

Great Clarendon Street, Oxford OX2 6DP
Text © Roderick Hunt and Annemarie Young 2007
Illustrations © Alex Brychta 2007
First published 2007
This edition published 2012

10 9 8 7 6 5 4 3 2 1
Series Editors: Kate Ruttle, Annemarie Young
British Library Cataloguing in Publication Data available
ISBN: 978-0-19-848796-8
Printed in China by Imago
The characters in this work are the original creation of Roderick Hunt and Alex Brychta who retain copyright in the characters.